SpongeBob had made the front page of the *Bikini Bottom News*. He squinted at the headline. "'LOCAL NUTCASE TRIES TO FLY,'" he read aloud.

SpongeBob reddened with anger. "I'm a nutcase because I follow my dreams?" He stabbed the air with his finger. "Well, they laughed at the guy who invented lightbulbs too."

"No, they didn't," replied the clerk.

SpongeBob looked momentarily defeated.

"You'll see," promised SpongeBob, making a fist. "I'll show everyone!"

SpongeBob AirPants: The Lost Episode

SpongeBob AirPants: The Lost Episode

adapted by **Kitty Richards**

based on the teleplay, "Volcano Pants,"

by **Merriweather Williams**

illustrated by **Heather Martinez**

SCHOLASTIC INC.

New York Toronto London Auckland Sydney
Mexico City New Delhi Hong Kong Buenos Aires

Based on the TV series *SpongeBob SquarePants*®
created by Stephen Hillenburg as seen on Nickelodeon®

ISBN 0-439-46392-0

12 11 10 9 8 7 6 5 4 3 2 1   3 4 5 6 7 8/0

Printed in the U.S.A.

First Scholastic printing, September 2003

Look for these other
SpongeBob SquarePants
chapter books!

SpongeBob AirPants: The Lost Episode

prologue

Last week a never-before-seen episode of SpongeBob SquarePants was discovered at Nickelodeon Studios. The world is waiting in anticipation to watch "SpongeBob SquarePants: The Lost Episode." Here to present the lost episode, from Encino, California, the president of the SpongeBob SquarePants fan club—Patchy the Pirate . . .

Patchy poked his head out from behind a flowered shower curtain. "Ahoy there, kiddies!" he said, his voice garbled by the sound of running water. "I'm just takin' me shower!"

Patchy wore a shower cap over his skull-and-crossbones pirate hat, and a patch over one eye. Soap bubbles clung to his scruffy beard.

"Uh, what are you all doing here?" he asked. Patchy smiled to reveal his missing tooth.

Patchy's loyal parrot, Potty, swooped onto the curtain rod. "They're here to see the lost episode," explained Potty.

Patchy looked worried. "B-b-but I haven't got the lost episode because I . . ." Patchy paused to gulp. "Lost it," he finished. Then he started to cry. "It's lost!" Patchy sobbed. "So it's best if you forget all about good old SpongeBob SquarePants!"

Once Patchy was dried off and dressed he sat on the couch, screwing on his peg leg. "I can't believe I lost the lost episode," he said with a sigh. "I never lose anything."

"What about your leg?" asked Potty.

Patchy shrugged. "Well . . . yeah," he admitted.

"And your eye," added Potty.

"And the eye," Patchy said.

"And your hand," Potty continued.

Patchy examined his hook then shot the parrot a dirty look. "Oh, get out of here you blasted bird!" he shouted.

"If only I could remember where I lost the lost episode." Patchy stood up and folded his arms across his chest.

Suddenly there was the sound of squealing brakes and—*crash*! Something flew through the living-room window, hitting Patchy right in the nose and knocking him to the ground.

"What is it?" asked Potty excitedly.

"It's a videotape!" Patchy said in disbelief. "It's the lost episode of *SpongeBob* I lost!"

The videotape was cleverly labeled SPONGEBOB: THE LOST EPISODE.

"It's a dream come true," said Potty.

Patchy ran into his kitchen and returned to the living room carrying an armful of snack food. He set the snacks down on the end table next to his La-Z-Pirate.

"Popcorn! Soda! Pickled garlic! Hurry, Potty! Hit the remote!" Patchy cried. "This is gonna be great! I can't believe it! Never-before-seen *SpongeBob*!"

Patchy shook the bag of popcorn and kernels flew everywhere. "This is so exciting! Here it comes!"

The video began to play. "And now . . . ," said the TV announcer, "the lost episode . . ."

chapter one

It was a beautiful day in Bikini Bottom. The water was pleasantly warm and the sun was shining brightly above the surface.

SpongeBob stood poised on a rolling green hill, jellyfish net in hand, staring in awe at the spectacle of dozens of beautiful translucent jellyfish floating all around him.

SpongeBob's fingers tightened around the net's handle. How he wanted to catch one!

A lone jellyfish, possibly the most beautiful specimen SpongeBob had ever seen, hovered nearby.

In a flash SpongeBob fashioned his body into a spring and bounded after the jellyfish. The jellyfish paused for a moment, and so did SpongeBob, net cocked over his head.

Suddenly SpongeBob looked down. He was no longer poised on a rolling green hill. Instead he was standing on—nothing! SpongeBob's springlike body uncoiled and he plummeted down, head first. *Kaplunk!*

"Oww!" SpongeBob moaned, rubbing his head.

SpongeBob looked up to see a single jellyfish swimming by, then a school of them silhouetted against the sunlight. He was awestruck.

"I salute you, oh, majestic jellyfish," SpongeBob began. "Your command of the sky is unmatched. Floating just out of the reach of my net, but near enough that I can see your untamed beauty."

Seized by a moment of pop-star inspiration SpongeBob burst into song:

If only I could join you there in the air,
Floating free without a care.
I wish I could fly
And see things with a different eye.
I would fly so very high and touch the sky
And never have to ask why it is that I
    can't fly . . .

His reverie was interrupted by a memory of something his grandfather had always told him. "Wait a minute," SpongeBob said. "I'm forgetting the famous last words of Grandpa SquarePants."

He envisioned his grandpa, cane in hand, saying, "If we were meant to fly, we'd have propellers on our heads or jet engines on our backs." Then Grandpa disappeared.

SpongeBob snapped his fingers. "That's it! I'm gonna follow Grandpa SquarePants's advice, by gum," he decided. "I'll invent a flying machine!"

chapter two

SpongeBob dressed himself in an old-fashioned aviator's outfit and set to work. In no time he had created a makeshift airplane, propeller and all.

SpongeBob stood in front of Farmer Jenkins's barn and grain silo, tightening a bolt on the wing just as his best friend, Patrick Star, showed up.

"What are you working on, SpongeBob?" Patrick asked.

"This, Patrick, is a flying machine," said SpongeBob proudly.

"Uh-huh. Uh-huh. Uh-huh," Patrick laughed out loud.

"What's so funny, Patrick?" SpongeBob wanted to know.

Patrick looked at his friend. "Everyone knows that if you were meant to fly, you'd have a propeller on your head or a jet engine on your back!"

SpongeBob thought for a moment. Where had he heard that before, he wondered.

"Well, here I go, Patrick," he said, running to the front of the plane. "I'm off to fly with the jellyfish!"

"Ignition, check!" SpongeBob cried, twisting the propeller. "Landing gear, check!" he shouted, kicking the tires. "Complimentary peanuts, check-a-roo!" he cried, waving a foil-wrapped packet in the air.

SpongeBob put on his aviator's goggles and hopped into the cockpit. "Ready for takeoff. Three . . . two . . . one . . ." *Clunk!*

Immediately the plane fell to pieces. SpongeBob landed on the ground next to where Patrick was standing, but the propeller kept going and going, slicing a hole right through a nearby silo. Grain rained down on SpongeBob and Patrick.

"You cut a hole in Farmer Jenkins's grain silo!" said Patrick through a mouthful of grain.

"Don't remind me," mumbled SpongeBob.

Farmer Jenkins heard the commotion and stormed over to the heap of spilled grain. "I knew no good would come from city folk and their flying machines. Now git!"

"We better do what he says," said Patrick as he scrambled to his feet. "He knows how to grow food."

"Well, it took me all night," said SpongeBob the next morning, clutching some rolled-up papers in his hand. "But here they are! The new blueprints! I wasn't even close with the designs for the last flying machine. Propellers, rudders, who needs them?" he said dismissively.

Soon after SpongeBob stood on the edge of a cliff clad in an elaborate bat suit—ears, wings, and all. "This one's gonna fly, I can feel it. Ready, Patrick?"

"Ready!" replied Patrick.

SpongeBob leaped into the air and hovered

for a moment, beating his big, black wings. "It's working Patrick. I'm flying!" He beat them faster and faster, but to no avail.

SpongeBob hung in the air for a moment and then plummeted down. "I'm falling! I'm falling! Aaaaaaah!" he screamed before slamming into the ground.

Patrick ran over and sprayed him with a fire extinguisher. Just in case.

A few hours later SpongeBob returned to his takeoff spot.

"This is it, Patrick," he announced, clipboard in hand. "The physics are solid. This time I'm really gonna fly! Behold . . ." He motioned to a lawn chair with two balloons tied to it.

"Oh, boy!" Patrick cried, throwing his arms in the air. "A birthday party!"

"No, Patrick," SpongeBob explained. "This is SquarePants Flyer Mark III. All you do is remove the brick weighing down the chair and . . ." He picked up the brick, but when he turned back around, his flying machine had taken off without him!

"Oh, barnacles!" SpongeBob cried. "Well, back to the drawing board."

"Can we have the cake now?" Patrick asked hopefully. "Happy birthday to me . . ."

The next day SpongeBob had readied his latest flying machine for takeoff.

"Patrick, get ready to say 'Eureka!'" said SpongeBob.

A rope was tied around his middle and he was attached to a big, red kite. The kite was attached to Patrick's pink tricycle below.

"Okay!" said Patrick. "Ready when you are!"

"Ready!" yelled SpongeBob.

Patrick started pedaling as hard as he could. He rode faster and faster until SpongeBob slowly rose straight into the air!

"It's working! I'm flying!" cried SpongeBob gleefully.

SpongeBob soared above three fish standing by the side of the road.

"Hey, look at that guy tied to a kite!" one of the fish cried, pointing at SpongeBob.

The other two looked puzzled. "Why is he doing that?" shouted the second fish.

"Oh, my goodness!" cried the third fish. "But he doesn't have a propeller on his head

or a jet pack on his back!"

SpongeBob looked down at the confused faces below. "Do not be afraid, earthbound beings," he said consolingly. "I am not a flying monster. I'm just one of you!"

Suddenly the kite snapped closed and SpongeBob plunged to the ground. Patrick kept pedaling on, unaware. SpongeBob was bounced repeatedly on the ground and dragged behind the tricycle.

"Ooooof! Pat-rick! Stop! Oohhh! Pat-rick! Oof!" cried SpongeBob.

The three fish laughed and laughed.

chapter three

SpongeBob marched straight to the store that had sold him the kite. "Excuse me, sir," he said, slapping the kite remnants on the counter. "I'd like to return this kite."

"Hey, I know you," said the clerk.

"Yeah," said a customer. "I saw you in today's paper."

SpongeBob had made the front page of the *Bikini Bottom News*. He squinted at the

headline. "'LOCAL NUTCASE TRIES TO FLY,'" he read aloud.

SpongeBob reddened with anger. "I'm a nutcase because I follow my dreams?" He stabbed the air with his finger. "Well, they laughed at the guy who invented lightbulbs too."

"No, they didn't," replied the clerk.

SpongeBob looked momentarily defeated.

"You'll see," promised SpongeBob, making a fist. "I'll show everyone!"

Walking down the street, SpongeBob passed a little boy fish in a propeller beanie hat who was holding his mother's hand.

"Look, Mommy, it's the Birdman of Bikini Bottom," said the boy fish.

"Well, I wonder why he's still using his legs," scoffed the mom.

"C'mon, birdman," taunted the boy fish. "Flap your wings and fly."

He and his mom snickered.

"Hey, Birdman!" called a fish in a baseball cap. "Going to check on your eggs?"

"Maybe he's looking for a statue to poop on!" said a girl fish with a giggle.

SpongeBob walked on and tried to stay calm, but he was becoming madder and madder all the while.

Another fish popped up right in front of him, flapping his fins and making chicken noises. A crowd had gathered and everyone joined together teasing SpongeBob.

"Go on and laugh," cried SpongeBob. "It is a sad day in Bikini Bottom when a guy is made fun of for having dreams!"

Two fish wearing bedroom slippers and

carrying triplets glowered at him. "You think you're the only one with unfulfilled dreams?" asked the mom fish, her hair in curlers.

"I was supposed to be a concert pianist," a fish with a five o'clock shadow said sadly. "Until I realized I didn't have any fingers." He held up his clublike fins.

"We all had dreams," pronounced a sullen-looking fish.

"What makes *you* so special?" asked another.

The crowd was getting worked up.

"Let's get him!" they shouted, chasing SpongeBob to a nearby cliff. SpongeBob looked left and then right. There was nowhere for him to go. He teetered at the edge. Then SpongeBob lost his balance and fell toward the ground.

"Good riddance, dreamer!" cried one of the fish.

Splat! SpongeBob landed in the back of a truck full of sticky mud. He was dirty, but unharmed. Then the truck turned a sharp corner and SpongeBob flew out. Covered in mud, he landed in the bed of another truck.

"Well, it can't get any worse," SpongeBob said optimistically, until he realized that he had landed in a truck full of feathers! "I guess I spoke too soon."

So SpongeBob had to walk all the way home completely covered in mud and feathers. Everyone who he passed laughed and pointed.

A reporter fish holding a camera followed him. "Say cheese, birdman!" he said and snapped his picture.

SpongeBob looked defeated. He started to say something in his defense, but instead he took a deep breath and let out a loud *"BAAAAAWK!"*

chapter four

The next morning SpongeBob stood inside his pineapple house after his morning bath, his head wrapped in a towel.

He looked out of his porthole window at the beautiful jellyfish floating outside.

"So close and yet so far!" SpongeBob sighed. "I suppose I'll never join them in the sky, Gary," he said to his pet snail. "I'll be stuck on the ground sentenced to a flightless life."

He removed the towel around his waist to reveal a pair of tighty whities. "Oh well, I guess all dreams aren't meant to come true." He pulled his clothes on in one motion. "Back to reality."

"Meow," said Gary, sympathetically.

"No, Gary," replied SpongeBob. "My dreams are silly." He took off his head towel and began to blow dry his head.

Just then his shell phone began to ring. SpongeBob tucked the still-blowing dryer into the waistband of his pants and answered the phone.

"Hello? No, this isn't the Birdman of Bikini Bottom. What? No, I certainly do not live in a birdcage!"

Irritated by the prank caller, SpongeBob did not notice that the dryer was causing his pants to fill with air.

As Gary looked on, SpongeBob's trousers began to inflate to enormous size. As the clothing expanded, Gary ducked into his shell. SpongeBob began to rise off the ground.

Brrring! The telephone rang again.

"Who is this?" SpongeBob asked the caller. "Joe Mama? Well, listen up, Joe, I hate to break it to you, but flying is impossible. I have to go now. My head just hit the ceiling." *Boing!*

"Huh? Hey! Look, Gary, I think I'm flying!" he cried. "Jellyfish Fields, here I come!"

The top of his pineapple house opened and SpongeBob floated up, up, and away.

He floated past Squidward's home and the Krusty Krab.

"Come down from there, SpongeBob!" called Mr. Krabs. "Ya can't flip me krabby patties from the sky!"

But SpongeBob continued to float away.

"Mom, look!" cried the boy fish in the funny cap. "It's the flying guy!"

"Wow! I guess he wasn't a lunatic after all," admitted the mom.

"Look at me! I'm flying! I'm flying!" shouted SpongeBob.

SpongeBob's miraculous flight inspired his fellow sea creatures to burst into song:

"He's flying! He's flying! He's really, really flying," they harmonized.

SpongeBob grinned and sang, *"I'd love to hang around to say I told you so. But it's off to Jellyfish Fields I go! Roads and streets are not for me."*

Suddenly SpongeBob heard a singing cry for help.

"Help, please help! My snail is up a tree!

I've had her since I was a little girl, but now it looks like the end of her world," sang Mrs. Puff, SpongeBob's boating school teacher.

The branch snapped and the little snail began to fall. "Noooooo!" cried Mrs. Puff. SpongeBob swooped forward and caught the snail, just in time.

"Gotcha!" said SpongeBob. "Next time try the elevator."

"Thank you, Birdman!" cried Mrs. Puff.

SpongeBob flew off, gliding through the air with glee. He began to sing again:

"I have never felt so free,
High in the sky is the place for me.
Helping friends from up above,
These are the things I love."

"*I'll help Mr. Krabs reclaim a dime,*" SpongeBob continued, handing Mr. Krabs a ten-cent piece.

"I'm rich!" cried Mr. Krabs, clutching the coin in his claw.

SpongeBob looked down. "*And I'll save Patrick from this mime!*"

Patrick stood, confused, in front of a street performer who was trapped inside an invisible box. SpongeBob swooped down to rescue him.

"Thanks, buddy," said Patrick gratefully.

SpongeBob pointed to a bunch of kelp moving back and forth.

"*Even Plankton needs some help.*
When he gets tangled in the kelp."

SpongeBob grabbed the one-eyed organism and plucked him from the kelp bed.

"Please put me down," Plankton said crossly.

On TV that night the *Bikini Bottom News* anchor stated, "All of Bikini Bottom is abuzz over the identity of a mysterious flying man who helps people."

"He found my hairpiece," said a fish wearing a very shiny black wig. It was obviously *not* his natural color.

A little boy fish appeared next. "He helps people and . . . he flies, and . . . he helps people," he babbled.

"Who knows what superhero act of courage he'll astound us with next!" said the anchor.

chapter five

On the coast a lighthouse beacon shorted out,
going black.

"Oh, no! The light in the Goo Lagoon
Lighthouse went out and Sailor Jenkins is
headed for the coastline!" a fish shouted.

"I'm glad I gave up farming!" shouted Sailor
Jenkins, formerly known as Farmer Jenkins,
from the deck of his boat. He was clad in a
fisherman's raincoat and rain hat.

"I'm coming!" called SpongeBob. Quick as a wink he unscrewed the old lightbulb and replaced it with a new one. He flipped the switch and the lighthouse flashed on.

Sailor Jenkins turned the boat around, safely heading back out to sea.

The crowd voiced its approval. "Hooray! Thanks, mysterious flying man!" they cheered.

Just then Sailor Jenkins drove his boat right into a titanic rock.

"I . . . I . . . I knew no good would come from city folk and their flying machines!" he spluttered.

"That's enough good deeds for one day!" said SpongeBob, brushing off his hands. "I've got a date with a group of jellyfish."

But Mr. Krabs stopped him in his tracks. "SpongeBob!" he cried. "Son, I need you and your magical pants!"

"But Mr. Krabs," said SpongeBob "I invented these pants so I could fly with the jellyfish. If I keep doing favors for people, I'll never get to make my dreams come true." He began to walk away.

"But SpongeBob," said Mr. Krabs. "It's an emergency!"

An emergency? SpongeBob knew when he was needed. He instantly inflated his flying pants, ready for action.

"Alrighty," SpongeBob said. "Let's fly!" He picked up his boss by the claws and took off into the air. "Where to, Mr. K?"

"Uh . . . my garage," Mr. Krabs replied.

"You got it!" said SpongeBob. They headed toward Mr. Krabs's anchor-shaped home and touched down.

"What's the emergency, Mr. Krabs?" SpongeBob asked.

Mr. Krabs looked SpongeBob squarely in the eye. "Are you sure you're up to it, boy?"

Sponge Bob nodded confidently. "I think my pants can handle it," he said.

"I need you . . . ," Mr. Krabs began.

"Yes?" said SpongeBob, leaning forward in anticipation.

"To clean . . . ," continued Mr. Krabs.

"Clean up crime?" SpongeBob guessed hopefully.

"My garage," finished Mr. Krabs.

SpongeBob's pants deflated at this news. "That's your emergency?" he asked.

"But SpongeBob!" said Mr. Krabs. "Everyone knows it's easier to clean a garage when you can fly."

SpongeBob thought about that for a moment. He had to admit Mr. Krabs had a point—it *was* easier to clean a garage when you could fly.

"Okay, Mr. Krabs," he agreed slowly. "I'll clean your garage, but after this, no more favors." He inflated his pants, ready to face the challenge.

A while later SpongeBob flew out of the garage looking slightly grimy, but still superhero-like. "All done, Mr. Krabs."

Mr. Krabs sat on a lawn chair, a sun reflector propped under his chin. "And the recyclables?" he asked.

SpongeBob's shoulder's sagged. "Ahh, tartar sauce!" he swore and turned back to the garage.

Once he finally finished the job SpongeBob

brushed himself off and cried out, "Jellyfish Fields, here I come!"

But then he heard something that made him stop in his tracks. "Help! SpongeBob!" shouted Patrick.

"Patrick's in trouble!" cried SpongeBob.

"SpongeBob! SpongeBob!" Patrick called again. He was lying flat on his back.

"What is it, buddy?" asked SpongeBob worriedly.

"Will you scratch my tummy?" asked Patrick.

SpongeBob was annoyed, but he did it anyway.

"Ahhhhh, right there!" said a very satisfied Patrick.

Suddenly everyone had an "emergency" for SpongeBob to help with.

"Help me pick out a tie," said Larry the

Lobster, displaying three colorful pieces of neckwear.

SpongeBob picked the flowered one.

"Clean my bathtub?" asked Squidward.

SpongeBob scrubbed away.

"Balance my checkbook?" asked Mrs. Puff.

SpongeBob did.

"Help spread the word of evil?" suggested Plankton.

SpongeBob handed out the Evil Inc. newsletter.

The requests started to come fast and furious. "Untangle my phone cord! Do my geometry! Talk to my plants! Rub my scalp!"

SpongeBob had had enough. "Wait a minute! Wait a minute! Wait a minute!" he cried, arms flailing. "I'm supposed to be at Jellyfish Fields right now! But instead I'm here rubbing your scalp—and I don't even know who you are!"

The fish look insulted. "But . . . we . . . went to elementary school together."

SpongeBob looked closer. "Is that you, Dennis?" he asked and began massaging his scalp once more.

Meanwhile the crowd was getting restless. "Where are you, SpongeBob? SpongeBob? Oh, SpongeBob! Hey, SpongeBob!" It seemed *everyone* had a favor to ask the man with the inflatable pants!

SpongeBob cowered behind a nearby rock. "If I don't give these feverish favor seekers the slip, I'll never get to fly with the jellyfish," he said. He decided to make a run for it.

"There he is!" someone shouted.

"He's getting away!" yelled someone else.

"No! He owes us favors!" the crowd shouted righteously.

"Get him!" cried the propeller-beanied boy. The crowd gave chase, hot on his heels until they got to a cliff.

"I'm almost to Jellyfish Fields!" said SpongeBob, panting. "I'm gonna make it!"

"He's headed for Jellyfish Fields! We'll never catch him now!" someone in the crowd cried disappointedly.

"I'll take care of this!" said Farmer/Sailor Jenkins. He stuffed himself into a cannon, only his helmeted head sticking out. The fuse was burning.

"Look! It's Cannonball Jenkins!" a fish cried.

Bang! Cannonball Jenkins flew through the air and collided with his target—SpongeBob and his amazing flying pants.

Kaboom! SpongeBob's pants exploded

and the two began to fall to the ground. Cannonball Jenkins released his parachute and landed gently as SpongeBob careened toward the hard ocean floor. *Thwack!* He lay spread-eagled, his clothing in tatters.

"I-I-I told ya nothing good would come from city folk and their flying machines," stammered Cannonball Jenkins.

The saddened crowd gathered around the fallen flying sponge. "What have we done?" said one of the fish, weeping. "C'mon, everybody. I think a proper burial is in order." He gently lifted up SpongeBob's trousers. "A pair of pants like this comes around once in a lifetime."

The crowd moved off leaving SpongeBob, sprawled on the ground wearing only his

tighty whities. After a short while SpongeBob came to and stood up.

"Well, it was fun while it lasted," said SpongeBob, dejectedly. "I guess I'm not meant to fly after all." He looked up at a jellyfish hovering nearby and sighed.

SpongeBob began to walk away, but he suddenly noticed that his legs weren't touching the ground! "What the? . . . ," he said. A group of jellyfish had slipped under his shoes, lifting him into the air!

"Hey! My jellyfish friends are helping me to fly—without pants!" the pants-less SpongeBob cried. "I guess it just goes to show . . ." SpongeBob's heart was so filled with joy that he began to sing:

"You don't need a plane to fly;
Plastic wings may make you cry.

Kites are made for windy days,
Lawn chairs with balloons fly away . . .
Inflatable pants . . . you may as well skip
If you want to fly . . .
All you need is friendship . . . yep!"

The jellyfish gently placed SpongeBob in front of his pineapple home. "Good-bye, jellies!" he cried, waving to his new friends. "You taught me a valuable lesson—although I'm not quite sure what it was."

Suddenly Patrick appeared from out of nowhere. "Hey, SpongeBob, let's fly down to the pizza place for a slice," he suggested.

SpongeBob shook his head. "No more flying for me, Patrick. I'll leave that to the jellyfish." He turned to go inside.

"Suit yourself," said Patrick, taking off into the air.

SpongeBob spun around. "Did Patrick just? . . . Nah!" SpongeBob laughed to himself and went inside. But two seconds later he opened his door to take a second look. . . .

The End

afterword

"Wow! Wasn't that great?" asked Patchy.

"Let's watch it again!" said Potty.

"That's a great idea, Potty." Patchy looked around. "Where's the remote? Oh no, I lost the remote! I can't believe I lost the remote!"

Suddenly something smashed through the window, knocking Patchy down.

"My remote!" Patchy cried happily. "Now which one of these cockamamy buttons is rewind?" he asked, fiddling with the remote control.

He started flipping through the channels. A juggling clown appeared on-screen. Then the weather. A cowboy movie. A football game. "No, that's not it," he said. "Wrong again."

"Squaaawk! Let me do it!" said Potty.

Potty landed on the remote and the lights went out.

"That's the light switch. Give me that," said Patchy. He hit another button and a festive three-piece band began to play.

"That's the Mariachi Band button," said Potty.

"I hate technology!" shouted Patchy. He kept hitting buttons. "Rewind, darn ye." The VCR began spitting out videotape all over the place.

"Stop! Stop! Oh, no! I've ruined The Lost Episode!" Patchy cried, wrapped in an enormous wad of videotape. "Now it's lost forever!"

"Squawk!" Potty flapped her wings and squawked loudly. "Lost forever!"